Rihanna

by C.F. Earl

Superstars of Hip-Hop

Rihanna

by C.F. Earl

Mason Crest

Rihanna

Mason Crest
370 Reed Road
Broomall, Pennsylvania 19008
www.masoncrest.com

Printed and bound in the United States of America.

First printing
9 8 7 6 5 4 3 2 1

          Library of Congress Cataloging-in-Publication Data

Earl, C. F.
  Rihanna / by C.F. Earl.
        p. cm. – (Superstars of hip-hop)
  Includes index.
  ISBN 978-1-4222-2526-4 (hard cover) – ISBN 978-1-4222-2508-0 (series hardcover) – ISBN 978-1-4222-2552-3 (soft cover) – ISBN 978-1-4222-9228-0 (ebook)
  1. Rihanna, 1988–-Juvenile literature. 2. Singers–Biography–Juvenile literature. I. Title.
  ML3930.R44E27 2012
  782.42164092–dc23
  [B]
                              2011020113

Produced by Harding House Publishing Services, Inc.
www.hardinghousepages.com
Interior Design by MK Bassett-Harvey.
Cover design by Torque Advertising & Design.

Publisher's notes:
• All quotations in this book come from original sources and contain the spelling and grammatical inconsistencies of the original text.
• The Web sites mentioned in this book were active at the time of publication. The publisher is not responsible for Web sites that have changed their addresses or discontinued operation since the date of publication. The publisher will review and update the Web site addresses each time the book is reprinted.

DISCLAIMER: The following story has been thoroughly researched, and to the best of our knowledge, represents a true story. While every possible effort has been made to ensure accuracy, the publisher will not assume liability for damages caused by inaccuracies in the data, and makes no warranty on the accuracy of the information contained herein. This story has not been authorized nor endorsed by Rihanna.

Contents

Hip-Hop lingo

Prejudice is judging someone unfairly because of race, religion, sex, or something else.

A **producer** is the person in charge of putting together songs. A producer makes the big decisions about the music.

An **audition** is when a person sings or performs for someone to see if that person likes her work and wants to give her a job.

Chapter 1

Beginnings in Barbados

Today, Rihanna is one of the world's most popular singers. Her songs are hits in countries across the globe. When Rihanna puts out new music, the whole world knows it. She's sold millions of albums and had many hit songs.

Rihanna is famous around the world. But she wasn't always so well known. Rihanna started her life far from the heights she'd reach in music. She was once a young girl with a dream of making it big.

Early Life

Robyn Rihanna Fenty was born on February 20, 1988, on the Caribbean island of Barbados. Like most Caribbean islands, Barbados is a sunny and beautiful place. There are many beaches. People come from all over the world to relax and enjoy themselves there. But for Rihanna, it was simply home.

Rihanna's mom, Monica Fenty, was an accountant. She also co-owned a small clothing store. Rihanna's dad, Ronald Fenty, worked at a factory that made clothes. Her mom was from Guyana, a small country in South America. Her dad was both African and Irish. Both her parents, however, grew up in Barbados. So they both called themselves Barbadians or "Bajan."

Growing up, Rihanna's dad struggled with drug addiction. He and Rihanna's mom fought a lot. Drugs only made things worse. Sometimes the fights got out of control. Then Rihanna would try to break them up. She tried to bring peace to the home. Sometimes it worked but never for long.

Today, Rihanna gives her mom credit for keeping her kids away from their father's drug habit. Rihanna didn't always know what was going on. She didn't always understand why her parents were fighting. But she knew it had something to do with drugs. Rihanna later told *Giant* magazine about those days: "I just knew that my mom and dad would always argue when there was a foil paper with an ashtray. He would just go to the bathroom all the time. I didn't know what it was. I really did not know. I just thought it was normal. Then one day, I heard them arguing about it. Then he did it again. And I told her. I said, 'Mom, he did that ashtray thing again.'"

This went on for years. Rihanna's parents split up many times during her childhood. Monica would kick Ronald out of the house, only to let him back in again.

Too Much for One Kid

Like any normal kid, it hurt Rihanna to grow up around so much fighting. But she never showed her pain to the world. She went to school every day with a smile on her face. She never cried or acted out in class or at home. So when she started to get really bad headaches, no one knew what was wrong.

At first, her mom thought Rihanna had a brain tumor. She was terrified! At the age of eight, Rihanna had to have a lot of tests.

Rihanna grew up on the beautiful island of Barbados in the Caribbean.

But doctors found nothing wrong with Rihanna's brain. Stress was making her head hurt, not a tumor.

For Rihanna's parents, this was a wakeup call. Their daughter needed them to be at peace. Monica would not let Ronald see his children until he got off drugs. So he made a hard choice. Rihanna told *Giant*, "My dad saw that what was between him and us was the drugs. He knew that to get closer to us, he had to cut that out. And he did."

Rihanna's dad had to put his life back together before he could be a good father for Rihanna.

Things still weren't great, though. When Rihanna was fourteen years old, her mom was fed up. She decided to end the marriage and get a divorce. "At that point, it was more of a relief," Rihanna told *Giant*.

After her parents' divorce, and after her dad stopped using drugs, Rihanna's head stopped hurting.

The Color of Her Skin

School was not a safe place for Rihanna to escape her problems. In fact, kids were very mean to her when she was young. In grade school, Rihanna often faced racism because of her skin color. In Barbados, where most people have dark skin, Rihanna's light skin really stood out. For the first six years of school, she went home every day feeling very upset.

Barbados is an island of many different peoples. Africans, Latinos, white Europeans, and Asians all live on the very small island. To say some people are "white" and others are "black" wouldn't be quite right. There are many different shades of skin color. But there are more people with dark skin. Lighter-skinned people can sometimes face **prejudice**.

Rihanna became a loner. She had very few friends. She got tough during those years. She didn't let her classmates' mean words bother her. And she also began to discover the things she really loved to do. As it turned out, one of those things was singing. But like any teenager without friends, she was lonely.

A New Friend and a New Start

Then one day, a girl named Melissa came to school. She changed everything for Rihanna. With Melissa, Rihanna didn't feel so alone anymore. The two girls quickly became best friends. They saw the world in the same way. They both had similar dreams.

Rihanna told *You* magazine about meeting Melissa for the first time: "When Melissa arrived at school she really stood out. She was a black girl with blonde hair who wore makeup—she was the only girl in school who would wear makeup, because we weren't allowed. We became friends and she would come over to my house with her older sister's magazines and we would go through them and say, 'Hey, we could do something like that.' That's when I started to get into fashion and makeup."

Rihanna went from having no friends to having one best friend. And that was all she needed. In high school, Rihanna really started to shine. She won a few beauty pageants. And, more important, she began to improve her music skills.

Rihanna's Big Break

Rihanna and two other girls started a singing group. They wanted to be like Destiny's Child and other groups that had made it big in the music business.

Then, one day, Rihanna got the phone call that changed her life. A friend told her that a famous music **producer**, Roger Evans, was visiting Barbados. Evans' wife was from Barbados. He loved to spend time on the island. He agreed to let Rihanna and her two friends **audition** for him.

When the three girls showed up at Evans's beach house, they'd never been more nervous. But Rihanna was ready for anything. She'd prepared a Destiny's Child song called "Emotion." Rogers couldn't believe what he was seeing or hearing. "The minute Rihanna walked into the room, it was like the other two girls didn't exist," he told *Entertainment Weekly*. "She carried herself like a star

This is the house where Rihanna grew up on Barbados.

even when she was fifteen. But the killer was when she opened her mouth to sing!"

And just like that, Rihanna's music career had begun. Evans knew he had a young star in Rihanna. Rihanna and her mom spent the next year flying back and forth between Barbados and Evans' house in the United States. Evans helped her train her voice. He wanted her to be ready for the big time.

Once Rihanna left Barbados, she was headed into a new chapter of her life.
She never looked back!

When she turned sixteen, Evans invited Rihanna to come live with his family in Connecticut. This time, when she went to America, she would stay there.

Flying high above the Caribbean Sea, Rihanna was headed toward an unknown future. She was still a teenager. She would be living far away from her family, her home country, and her friends. But she had a smile on her face. "When I left Barbados, I didn't look back," Rihanna told *Entertainment Weekly*. "I wanted to do what I had to do [to succeed], even if it meant moving to America."

It was time to get to work on her dream.

Hip-Hop lingo

A **studio** is a place where musicians go to record their music and turn it into CDs.

A **demo** is a rough, early version of a CD before the real thing comes out.

Labels are companies that produce music and sell CDs.

A **contract** is a written agreement between two people. Once you've signed a contract, it's against the law to break it. When a musician signs a contract with a music company, the musician promises to give all her music to that company for them to produce as CDs and then sell—and the music company promises to pay the musician a certain amount of money. Usually, a contract is for a certain period of time.

Reggae is a type of music that started in Jamaica. It has a strong beat and combines different types of music, such as blues, jazz, and rock.

The **singles chart** is a list of the best-selling songs for a week.

Tours are when a musician travels around and plays music for people at concerts.

Mentors are people who teach someone else life lessons.

Chapter 2

Making It Big in America

Not many kids could have done what Rihanna did when she was only sixteen years old. But she wanted music to be her life. While other kids were going on dates or playing sports, Rihanna was in the **studio**. She came to America for one reason: to make music. There wasn't much time for doing anything else.

Living With the Rogers Family

Evan Rogers had a plan for Rihanna. He wanted her to move to America and make a four-song **demo**. The demo would then be sent around to music **labels**. If a company liked Rihanna's music, it would offer her a **contract**. That's how the music business worked. And no one knew the music business better than Evan Rogers.

Evan had had his own career as a singer. He was a member of a group called Rhythm Syndicate. They had a few hits in the early 1990s. Later on, Evan and one of his bandmates, Carl Sturken, started

Rihanna is the person she is today
partly because of the Rogers' influence in her life.

writing songs for other artists. They made hit songs for stars like Christina Aguilera and Kelly Clarkson.

Rihanna called him "Uncle Evan." Even today, after all her success, she is thankful for his help in those early days. Evan wanted to make Rihanna's move to America as easy as possible. He wanted her to feel like she had a new home.

Evan's wife, Jackie, is from Barbados. She knew where Rihanna was coming from. She understood how lonely Rihanna must feel. Jackie acted like a mother to the young girl. She got Rihanna a tutor so she could finish high school. She helped her keep her life together. Rihanna told *Giant* how thankful she was for Jackie during those years. "She took care of me when I was there. She made sure I had my laundry done. She made sure I ate on time."

Jackie and the rest of the Rogers family made it easier for Rihanna to relax in the studio. She could focus on making her first hit song.

In the Studio

Those were exciting days for Rihanna. She was growing as both a woman and a singer. Evan Rogers told *Giant* that Rihanna's voice was unlike anyone else's. "She was a little rough around the edges, but her voice was unique and full of potential."

The more time Rihanna spent in the studio, the better that voice became. She recorded four songs for her demo. One of them, "Pon de Replay," would become her first hit.

A demo CD has a few samples of the artist's music. If a label likes an artist's demo, it agrees to make her full-length CD. Evan Rogers' job was to find a label for Rihanna. Once he felt like the demo was good enough, he mailed it to labels across the country.

A Meeting with Def Jam

Def Jam Records was one of the best labels in hip-hop. And in 2005, Def Jam also had one of the best rappers in the game as its president—Jay-Z. When Jay-Z heard Rihanna's demo, he knew she had something special. He invited her to Def Jam's studio in New York City for an audition.

Rihanna couldn't believe it was true. When she arrived at the studio, she was shaking. This was her big moment. Her chance to be a star. Then she saw spotted Jay-Z walking into the audition room. "I saw just a little bit of Jay's face down the hall and I was just like, 'Oh my God!' I had never met a celebrity, and to meet a celebrity who's also the president of the label, that was crazy!" Rihanna told *Singer Universe*.

But Rihanna kept her cool. She sang her heart out. Jay-Z and the other Def Jam big shots were very impressed. They decided they couldn't wait another day to sign this talented singer. So they signed the deal right there, on the spot. Rihanna told *Singer Universe*, "We were there until 4:30 in the morning closing the deal. Every time I signed my name [on the contract], I was just smiling."

Caribbean Queen

Def Jam decided to put Rihanna's first album on the fast track. They wanted her album to come out in the summer of 2005. They called it *Music of the Sun*.

Plenty of other young female artists wanted to be stars. But Rihanna was different. She wasn't just another girl trying to be like Beyoncé. For starters, her Caribbean background helped set her apart. **Reggae** music was starting to make a comeback in the early 2000s. Rihanna was the perfect singer for the new style. Her voice was smooth and clear, with just a touch of a Caribbean accent.

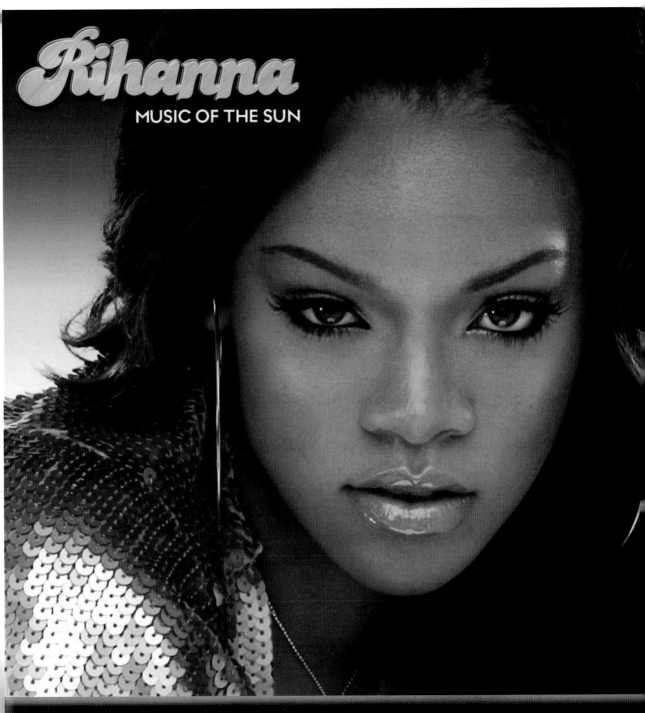

Rihanna's first album, *Music of the Sun*.

Most important, Rihanna had a hit song—"Pon de Replay." Jay-Z had taken her demo song and polished it for the radio. Before long, Rihanna's hit song was bumping in car stereos across the country.

"Pon de Replay" made it to number two on the **singles chart**. The song was a big hit around the world, too. The song could be heard on the radio and in clubs in many different countries. It helped make Rihanna a star. It also helped sell *Music of the Sun*. The album was a big success. It sold two million copies around the world.

Music of the Sun was a huge hit. Rihanna had become music's newest star. With a smash song and a big album, it seemed like there was no stopping the new star from Barbados.

Not Slowing Down

After making a hit album, many artists would take a break. But Rihanna did the opposite. She wanted to use *Music of the Sun*'s success to sell her next album. Just eight months after *Music of the Sun* came out, Rihanna made her second album. This one was called *A Girl Like Me*.

A Girl Like Me made Rihanna even more famous. The album had two hit songs! "SOS" and "Unfaithful" played on radios everywhere.

Why make a second album so soon? Because Def Jam wanted to make Rihanna's name famous. They wanted everyone to be talking about this new artist from Barbados. And it worked. People started to think of Rihanna as more than just another young Beyoncé. In the music world, stars rise and fall all the time. Rihanna was here to stay.

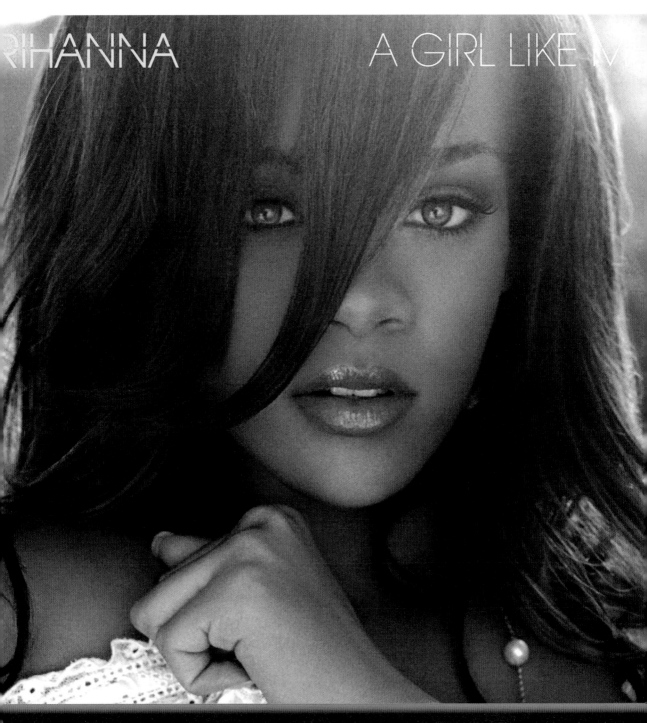

The album cover for Rihanna's second album, *A Girl Like Me*.

Jay-Z has played a big role in Rihanna's life.

Needing a Break

Making two albums in one year is very hard work. A singer's work doesn't end when her album goes to stores. There are **tours** and public speaking events. There are other things that take a lot of time and energy, too. So, after 2005, Rihanna was very tired.

Lucky for Rihanna, she had smart **mentors** like Jay-Z to give her good advice. Jay-Z told her she needed to take a break. He'd been in the music business for a long time. He knew young singers could get burnt out if they worked too hard without a break. So he told her to go home to Barbados. She could take a vacation, relax, and soak up some sunshine.

Rihanna took Jay-Z's advice and went home. She ate some home-cooked meals. She spent time at the beaches where she grew up. But she was soon ready to go back to the United States. Rihanna truly loved being a singer. She couldn't wait to get back to work and continue her career!

Hip-Hop lingo

Singles are songs that are sold by themselves.

Lyrics are the words in a song.

Each year, the National Academy of Recording Arts and Sciences gives out the **Grammy Awards** (short for Gramophone Awards)—or Grammys—to people who have done something really big in the music industry.

When someone's on **probation**, he doesn't have to go to prison as long as he obeys certain rules—such as not doing drugs or staying away from certain people.

A **role model** is someone whom kids can look up to and try to be like.

Chapter 3

Good Girl Gone Bad

Rihanna was growing up. She was only nineteen years old, but she had lived through more than many people older than her had! She had sold millions of albums. She'd been in the studio for weeks at a time. She'd had her makeup and hair done for hundreds of interviews. She was starting to feel like she was living someone else's life.

Her vacation in Barbados helped. But she still felt like she needed another change. For her entire career, Rihanna had let other people control her image. Hip-hop stars' images include a lot of things, like how they dress, how they do their hair and makeup, as well as what kinds of songs they choose to make. For her first two albums, Rihanna's image was a young, sweet girl. She had flowing brown hair. She always looked happy and innocent.

Rihanna wanted to be herself. She didn't want people to control her image anymore. She cut her hair short and dyed it black. And she didn't stop there. She also changed her music. It was a whole new Rihanna. And she wanted the world to know it. The title of her next album said it all: *Good Girl Gone Bad*.

A New Image

When Rihanna talks about being "bad," she doesn't mean doing bad things or treating others poorly. Being "bad" is about a change in attitude. Rihanna explained the title of her album to *Entertain-*

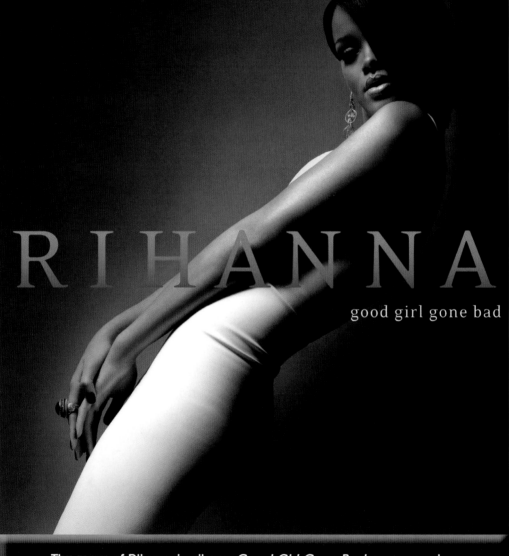

The cover of Rihanna's album, *Good Girl Gone Bad*, expresses her determination to do things her own way, whether people like it or not.

ment Weekly. "It's like, 'This is me. This is what I'm doing. I don't care if you like it or not.' That's a bad girl's attitude."

Rihanna began to make a lot of changes in her life. She moved out of the Rogers home. She got her own apartment in L.A. She started dressing in all black. In many ways, she was doing what a lot of teenagers do: rebelling. But Rihanna had good friends and good mentors to keep her head in the right place. Evan Rogers never stopped believing in Rihanna. He knew it was time for her to grow up and be her own woman.

And Jay-Z also supported her new image. But he also had some advice to give. He told *Entertainment Weekly,* "The biggest advice I can give her is to keep her circle tight, because she can't control anything else outside of that. She can't control people's opinion of her records or what's being said on blogs. . . . But if she has the proper friends, she won't get caught up in the wild-child lifestyle. They will bring her back and be like, 'You might wanna pull your skirt down.'"

Jay-Z's words turned out to be true. Rihanna did keep her circle of friends tight. And she didn't let fame go to her head. Tova Dann was one of Rihanna's friends in L.A. She told *Giant* that Rihanna acted like a mature adult. "There's no drinking, partying or going out late at night and being irresponsible. . . . I've never once seen her take a sip of alcohol because she's only nineteen. She respects the law here."

Good Girl Makes Rihanna a Superstar

Rihanna's new image and her new album were a bit hit. Her first two albums sold very well and made her famous. But *Good Girl Gone Bad* turned Rihanna into a superstar. There were eight hit **singles** on the album. That's a huge number for one album!

One song, "Umbrella," was a worldwide number-one hit. That means it was a number-one song in more countries than just the United States. In England, the song stayed at number-one for ten weeks. It broke all kinds of records.

"Umbrella" featured a verse by Jay-Z. Jay had shown Rihanna how to succeed in the music business. He'd helped her make it big. He'd given her the chance of a lifetime. Now, the two got to make a hit song together.

Her other singles included "Shut Up and Drive," "Don't Stop the Music," and "Hate That I Love You." They also sold very well. "Don't Stop the Music" was a number-one hit in countries around the world.

People loved Rihanna's new sound. Her songs kept people dancing. They had good **lyrics** too. Rihanna's hard work had paid off. At the 2008 **Grammy Awards**, she earned her first Grammy for the song "Umbrella." She and Jay-Z accepted the award together.

Rihanna was at the top of every chart, and everyone knew her name. It seemed like nothing could go wrong for the young star.

But then, in February of 2009, Rihanna's world came crashing down on her.

Rihanna and Chris Brown

Rihanna met Chris Brown when they were both still teenagers. Chris was actually one year younger than Rihanna. Like Rihanna, Chris was a talented singer and a rising star. The two quickly became friends. Before long, they started dating.

Later on, Rihanna described Chris as her best friend. She said that those early days with him were very happy. But their love soon became dangerous. On the show *20/20*, Rihanna told Diane Sawyer, "The more in love we became, the more dangerous we became for each other, equally as dangerous." Rihanna said their relationship

At first, Rihanna and Chris Brown were happy together—but then their relationship became dangerous.

became an "obsession." An obsession is when something becomes too important. A person with an obsession can't let it go; she thinks about it all the time. It wasn't a healthy relationship, and it came to a violent end.

A Violent Night

On February 8, 2009, Rihanna was supposed to sing at the Grammy Awards. Chris Brown was supposed to be her date. The two were dressed up and ready for a beautiful night. Chris rented a sports car to drive them to the show. They were on their way when they started to argue.

The argument was about a text message that Chris's ex-girlfriend had sent him. Chris lied about the message. Rihanna would not let him off the hook. The argument turned into a fight. That's when it happened.

Chris attacked Rihanna. She was able to get out of the car and walk away. But her face was swollen and bleeding. Someone heard her screams and called the police. When help finally arrived, Rihanna was a mess. She was dressed in a fancy evening gown, and she had a black eye.

Rihanna had no choice but to miss the Grammys. She wouldn't be doing any singing that night.

Learning from Mistakes

Chris Brown admitted he was guilty of attacking Rihanna. He was given five years of **probation**. Many people were very angry at Chris. They wanted to hurt him for what he did to Rihanna. So a month after the attack, Rihanna went to visit him. Even after what he did to her, Rihanna wanted to protect him.

She forgave Chris for the attack. But she didn't go back to being his girlfriend. She realized his violent actions were part of a

Rihanna took Chris to court after what happened between them, and Chris was sentenced to 180 days of community service, five years probation, and domestic violence counseling.

Chris Brown had his own history of abuse, just like Rihanna did. The couple needed to separate from each other so that they could each grow up some more.

dangerous pattern in both their lives. When she was a kid, Rihanna's dad had hit her mother. Rihanna would smash dishes or tug at her dad's pants, anything to make them stop fighting.

Chris had seen his mother beaten, too. His stepfather had hit his mother. Chris grew up hating him. He told *Giant* how scared their fights made him. Some nights, he would be too afraid to get out of bed and go to the bathroom. Chris said, "[My stepdad] made me terrified all the time, terrified like I had to pee on myself. I remember one night he made her nose bleed. I was crying and thinking, 'I'm just gonna go crazy on him one day.' I hate him to this day."

But Chris messed up, just like his stepfather. And Rihanna didn't want to be a part of that mess. So she decided to learn from her mistakes. She decided to be a good **role model** for kids. Violence is a reality for many teens in relationships. Rihanna wanted to let young women know that violence is never okay. Hurtful words and hurtful actions are not loving. No matter how much she thought she loved Chris, she realized she could not go back to him.

Hip-Hop lingo

When someone has been **nominated**, he has been picked as one of the people who might win an award.

A **collaboration** is when two or more people work together on a project.

Chapter 4

Rihanna Gets *Loud*

After leaving Chris Brown, Rihanna knew she had to move on. She also knew she had to express what she was feeling. She knew she had to get it out in her music. It was the best way for her to let others know how she felt. Rihanna went into the studio to start work on her next album.

Rated R

Rihanna's fourth album came out on November 20, 2009. It was called *Rated R.*

Rihanna wanted to bring a new sound to her new album. She wanted something really tough. She wanted to show people how different she could sound from *Good Girl Gone Bad.*

Rated R definitely showed a different side of Rihanna. The songs on the album had a darker sound than *Good Girl Gone Bad.* The first single from the album was called "Russian Roulette." The song was slower than some of her others. It had a big beat, but it wasn't really a dance song. "Russian Roulette" was more about Rihanna's voice. She sings about the risks of love. Her voice sounds strong on the song, but she also shows lots of emotion.

The song was a hit. It made it to number nine on the singles chart. It was Rihanna's fourth top-ten song since *Good Girl Gone Bad.*

The next single was called "Hard." The song had a low, rumbling sound. It featured Young Jeezy. On "Hard," Rihanna sings about being tough even when people try to tear others down. "Hard" also made it into the top ten on the singles chart.

Next, Rihanna put out "Rude Boy." The song was much easier to dance to than the first two singles. It had a thumping beat and a catchy chorus. The song had a much lighter sound than the early singles from *Rated R*. It made it to number one on the charts.

Rihanna's next two singles did well, too. "Rockstar 101" featured guitarist Slash. *Rated R*'s final single was "Te Amo."

Rated R was a huge success. The album sold more than 180,000 copies in its first week. *Rated R* has sold more than a million copies in the United States alone.

Rated R wasn't the only thing Rihanna worked on in 2009. She also did a song with Jay-Z and Kanye West called "Run This Town." Rihanna was featured on the chorus. Jay-Z put the song on his album *The Blueprint 3*.

At the 2010 Grammys, Rihanna was **nominated** for two awards for "Run This Town." She, Jay-Z, and Kanye were up for Best Rap Song and Best Rap/Sung **Collaboration**.

Rihanna was back on top of the world. She'd come a long way in just a year. She'd left behind the drama with Chris Brown. She stayed strong. She never let anyone keep her down. She didn't let anything people were saying get to her.

Rated R helped Rihanna show her fans a new side of herself. It also helped her stay on top of the music world. She was still one of music's biggest stars.

Loud

Rihanna didn't slow down any after *Rated R*. Just less than one year later, she was back with her fifth album. Its title was short and sweet. She called it *Loud*.

Rihanna told her fans she was moving her music forward. She said she didn't want to make *Good Girl Gone Bad* or *Rated R* again.

Just like before, Rihanna was changing her sound and her look. She dyed her hair bright red. On the cover of *Loud*, she wore bright red lipstick to match. Rihanna wanted to be herself on the new album, she told her fans. "That's when I feel best," she said.

Rihanna started working on *Loud* in February 2010. The album was done by the end of the summer.

Rated R gave Rihanna both a new sound and a new look. She wanted people to know she was tough!

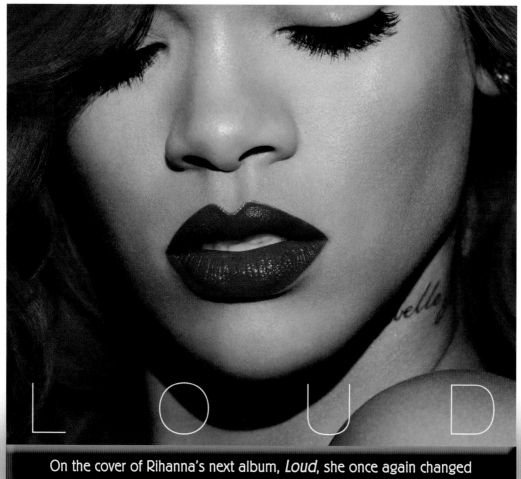

On the cover of Rihanna's next album, *Loud*, she once again changed her look.

While she was working on *Loud*, Rihanna also worked with rapper Eminem. Rihanna sang the chorus "Love the Way You Lie." Eminem put out the song on his 2010 album *Recovery*.

"Love the Way You Lie" was a huge hit. It turned out to be one of the biggest songs of the year. The song is about a relationship between two people that love each other but fight a lot. The lyrics were harsh. But they spoke to people who'd had to deal with what Rihanna's been through.

Loud was released on November 12, 2010. The album's first single came out in September. It was called "Only Girl in the World."

"Only Girl (In the World)" was a huge hit. It reached number one. It was a hit around the world, too.

After the dark songs of *Rated R*, "Only Girl" sounded bright and sunny. With its pounding bass and big chorus, the song was made for dancing. It was a big hit at clubs.

The next single was called "What's My Name?" The song featured Drake rapping a verse. "What's My Name?" was a bit slower than "Only Girl." But that didn't stop it from becoming a huge hit. "What's My Name?" reached number one, too.

Loud was a giant hit. The album sold 207,000 copies in its first week. It sold more copies in its first week than any of Rihanna's early albums. After just under two months, *Loud* had sold around 750,000 copies in the United States. The album was also a success around the world. It reached number one on the album charts in the UK, Canada, Norway, Scotland, and Switzerland.

At the end of 2010, Rihanna learned she'd been nominated for four Grammys. She was nominated for three awards for "Love the Way You Lie" and one for "Only Girl in the World." "Only Girl in the World" was nominated for Best Dance Recording. Rihanna's song with Eminem was up for Record of the Year, Best Music Video, and Best Rap/Sung Collaboration.

Talk That Talk

After the success of *Loud*, Rihanna kept working hard to bring her fans new music. In 2011, she toured the world, performing for fans in countries around the globe. In September, Rihanna put out a new song called "We Found Love." The song was the first single from her next album. "We Found Love" was a major hit. The song was on TV, on radio, and in clubs around the world.

In November, Rihanna released her sixth studio album, *Talk That Talk*. The album was a huge success for Rihanna. In its first week, the album sold just fewer than 200,000 copies in the United

At the 2011 Grammys, Rihanna's song "Only Girl in the World" won Best Dance Recording.

States. By the end of April 2012, the album had sold more than 850,000 copies in the United States.

Rihanna worked hard in 2011. She worked on her own music and worked with other artists like Coldplay and rapper Drake. But Rihanna was working on more than music during 2011. She was also acting in her first film. *Battleship*, Rihanna's first movie, was released in 2012. Rihanna said that she hoped to work on more movies after finishing *Battleship*.

In early 2012, Rihanna performed "We Found Love" at the Grammy Awards. After singing her hit single, Rihanna sang "Princess of China" with Coldplay. Later that night, Rihanna won a Grammy for her work on Kanye West's "All of the Lights." Rihanna had had another successful year, one of many for the superstar!

Looking to the Future

Rihanna has done more in her time in music than many do in a lifetime. Her hits aren't just hits in one country. They're played in countries across the globe. From "S.O.S." to "Umbrella" to "Only Girl in the World," Rihanna shows no sign of slowing down. With an ear for music and a great voice, Rihanna has reached millions of people.

Rihanna may be one of music's biggest stars today, but she's struggled to get there. She's had to deal with a lot of ups and downs. She's had great success in music. But she's also had to deal with many of the same issues as millions of others. Through it all, Rihanna has believed in herself. She's fought to be the best artist she can be.

After facing her personal problems in front of millions, nothing can stop Rihanna. Her music has kept people dancing for years. Her songs have brought people happiness. They've helped her fans stay strong through their own hard times.

There's no telling where Rihanna will go next with her music. She's changed her style and her sound more than once. Will she make another big change? We can only wait and see!

Time Line

1988   Robyn Rihanna Fenty is born in Saint Michael, Barbados.

2003   Rihanna meets record producer Evan Rogers.

2004   Rihanna wins her high school beauty pageant.

She moves to the United States to live with Evan Rogers and his family.

2005   Rihanna interviews with CEO Jay-Z. He signs her to Def Jam Records.

She releases her first single, "Pon de Replay."

She releases her first album, *Music of the Sun*. The album sells more than 2 million copies.

2006   Rihanna begins work on her second album, called *A Girl Like Me*.

The album's first single, *SOS*, goes to number one.

A Girl Like Me is released in April.

Rihanna creates the Believe Foundation to help sick children.

2007   Rihanna releases her third album, *Good Girl Gone Bad*.

The album's lead single, "Umbrella," is a world-wide hit.

2008   Rihanna wins her first Grammy award for "Umbrella."

2009   In February, Rihanna is attacked by her boyfriend, Chris Brown.

She releases her fourth album, *Rated R*.

2010   Rihanna wins two Grammy Awards for "Run This Town."

She releases her fifth album, *Loud*.

2011 Rihanna wins a Grammy for her song "Only Girl in the World." She goes on tour for the fourth time, the "Loud Tour."

Rihanna releases *Talk That Talk*.

2012 Rihanna appears in *Battleship*.

Discography
Albums

2005 Music of the Sun

2006 A Girl Like Me

2007 Good Girl Gone Bad

2009 Rated R

2010 Loud

2011 Talk That Talk

In Books

Baker, Soren. *The History of Rap and Hip Hop*. San Diego, Calif.: Lucent, 2006.

Comissiong, Solomon W. F. *How Jamal Discovered Hip-Hop Culture*. New York: Xlibris, 2008.

Cornish, Melanie. *The History of Hip Hop*. New York: Crabtree, 2009.

Czekaj, Jef. *Hip and Hop, Don't Stop!* New York: Hyperion, 2010.

Haskins, Jim. *One Nation Under a Groove: Rap Music and Its Roots*. New York: Jump at the Sun, 2000.

Hatch, Thomas. *A History of Hip-Hop: The Roots of Rap*. Portsmouth, N.H.: Red Bricklearning, 2005.

Websites

Official Rihanna Fan Site
www.rihannadaily.com

Official Rihanna Site
www.rihannanow.com

Rihanna on Internet Movie Database
www.imdb.com/name/nm1982597

Rihanna on MTV
www.mtv.com/music/artist/rihanna/artist.jhtml

Rihanna on MySpace
www.myspace.com/rihanna

Index

About the Author

C.F. Earl is a writer living and working in Binghamton, New York. Earl writes mostly on social and historical topics, including health, the military, and finances. An avid student of the world around him, and particularly fascinated with almost any current issue, C.F. Earl hopes to continue to write for books, websites, and other publications for as long as he is able.

Picture Credits

Def Jam Recordings: pp. 21, 23, 28, 39, 40
Fotolia, Photosite: p. 9
PR Photos: pp. 6, 14, 16, 18, 24, 26, 43

All other images are believed to be in the public domain. If the publisher has failed, however, to give proper credit for any image, please contact Harding House Publishing Services, 220 Front Street, Vestal, New York 13850, so that rectification can be made.